Iggy & Me

and the new baby

D0248246

Also by Jenny Valentine :

Iggy and Me

Iggy and Me and the Happy Birthday

Iggy and Me on Holiday

Jenny Valentine

Iggy & Me and the new baby

Illustrated by Joe Berger

HarperCollins *Children's Books*

First published in Great Britain by HarperCollins
Children's Books in 2012
HarperCollins Children's Books is a division of
HarperCollins Publishers Ltd
77-85 Fulham Palace Road, Hammersmith, London W6 8JB

www.harpercollins.co.uk

1

ISBN: 978-0-00-746354-1

Printed and bound in England by
Clays Ltd, St Ives plc

MIX
Paper from
responsible sources
FSC C007454

FSC™ is a non-profit international organisation established to promote
the responsible management of the world's forests. Products carrying the
FSC label are independently certified to assure consumers that they come
from forests that are managed to meet the social, economic and
ecological needs of present and future generations,
and other controlled sources.

Find out more about HarperCollins and the environment at
www.harpercollins.co.uk/green

Contents

Please May Can

My name is Flo and I have a little sister called Iggy. I am nine and Iggy is six. We are each other's only sister.

One morning, when we were walking to school, Iggy asked Mum a question.

She started with, "Please may can..."

I know that when Iggy uses all her polite words at once, she is really hoping for a 'yes'. She says, "Please may can we have an ice cream and a biscuit?" and "Please may can we go on a bike ride and a picnic and sleep in a tent?"

"Please may can we have a baby?" Iggy

asked, with her sweetest good-idea smile.

Mum slowed down, just a little bit.

"No, Iggy, I don't think so."

"How come?" said Iggy, and she looked a bit deflated, like an old balloon.

"Just because."

Iggy said that wasn't a reason.

"True," said Mum. "You've got me there."

"So why not?" Iggy asked, and then she added another, "Pleeease," with extra ee's, just to be on the safe side.

"I've had my babies," Mum said, and she took our hands, mine and then Iggy's. "*You*, and *you*."

"You can have more than *two* children." Iggy smiled, like that solved it.

"I know that." Mum smiled back.

Iggy told her, "Thomas Wilkes's mum has got *eight*."

"Nine," I said.

"*Nine?*" said Mum.

"Yes." I counted on my fingers. "Thomas, Ruby, Emma, James, Sophie, Will, Patrick, Sarah and Ben."

"Wow," said Mum. "Nine."

"James is in my class," I said, "and Thomas is in Iggy's. That's how we know. When they go to the supermarket, they have to buy nine of *everything*."

Iggy counted, "Nine toothbrushes, nine pairs of pants, nine packets of lemon drizzle cakes."

Iggy loves lemon drizzle cake.

I said, "The Wilkes's house is full of people and noise all the time, even when it's just them."

Mum frowned. "Well, Mr and Mrs Wilkes might have wanted nine children, but two is enough for me and your dad. That's what we decided. One under each arm in an emergency."

"What emergency?" I said.

Iggy was quiet for a minute. "You and Dad have got *four* arms. There's room for two more."

"Good Maths," Mum said, but she didn't tell me what the emergency was.

"Will you and Dad change your minds?"

Iggy said.

"No," said Mum. "Absolutely not," and she ruffled my hair and gave Iggy her school bag and kissed her goodbye on the nose.

Iggy doesn't do 'absolutely nots'. In Iggy's ears, an 'absolutely not' is *always* a 'maybe'.

When Mum says, "Absolutely not," about a thing, Iggy goes and asks Dad. And when Dad says, "Absolutely not," she double checks with Mum. Iggy thinks there's always a chance she'll get lucky. Sometimes she does.

So later, at suppertime, Iggy asked Dad the question too.

"Please may can you and Mum please have one or two more babies?"

Dad's mouth fell open. It was a bit full of supper.

"Ewww!" Iggy said, looking away and shielding her eyes with her hands. "Manners!"

Dad finished his mouthful. "I thought you were going to ask me to pass the salt or the butter. I didn't think you were going to ask for *babies*."

"Can you?" Iggy said. "Have one or two?"

"No," said Mum.

"We *can*," Dad said, "but we might not want to."

Iggy huffed with confusion. "What does that *mean*? Do you want to, or not?"

"Not," said Dad.

"Definitely not," said Mum.

"Please?" said Iggy.

"Abso*lutely* not," said Mum again.

"Let's talk about something else," said Dad. "How was your day, Flo? What did you learn at school?"

I started to tell Dad all about solids and liquids and gases, because that's what we've been doing in Science. Iggy was scowling into her soup, which is a liquid.

"I *want* one," she said.

"Well, you can have one of your own," Mum said. "When you're older."

"Yowch!" said Iggy. "I'm not doing that. Not *ever*."

Dad and Mum looked at each other and smiled.

"Maybe you'll change your mind," said Mum.

"No way," said Iggy, and she squeezed her eyes tight shut and shook her head.

"Oh well," said Dad, helping himself to more cauliflower. "No babies for you then. Never mind."

"Where were we?" Mum said. "What were you saying, Flo?"

"It's not *fair*," said Iggy, interrupting again, before I could even get started.

Not fair is Iggy's explanation for a lot of things.

When Mum says no to sweets, it's not fair.

When Iggy has to go to bed half an hour before me, it's not fair.

When we have rice and broccoli with our supper and Iggy wants chips and beans, it's not fair.

When Iggy decides we should go swimming and to the zoo and out for pizza and we don't because it's only a Wednesday and not anybody's birthday, it's not fair.

"Here we go," said Dad, and he rolled his eyes and winked at me.

"But I *really* want a little brother or sister," she moaned. "And it *really* isn't fair."

Dad said, "Flo's got a little sister, haven't you?"

"Yep," I said.

"How's that working out for you?" said Dad.

"So far so good," I said.

"*See.*" Iggy pointed at me. "Flo's got one. It's *so* not fair."

Mum stood up and cleared our plates away.

"Life isn't fair, Iggy," she said.

Iggy sighed and slumped forward with her forehead on the table. Her voice came out all squished and mumbly.

"I've *noticed*," she said.

In the playground at school, all Iggy could think about and talk about was babies.

She said, "Flo, what do babies smell like?" and "Why do some babies look like old men?" and "How many babies is it *possible* to have?"

"I don't know," I said.

"How many days does it take to grow a

baby?" and "Do babies have teeth?" and "Do *all* babies like mashed banana?"

"Iggy," I said, "*I don't know.*"

"Well, who does?" Iggy looked around the playground. "I need to find out."

"Why don't you ask James Wilkes?" I said. "He's got lots of baby brothers and sisters. He's probably an expert."

"Will you ask him?" Iggy said. "He's your friend."

"You're the one who wants to know," I said, "but I'll come with you."

So Iggy took me to find James Wilkes and quiz him about babies.

"What are they like?" Iggy said.

"Smelly," said James Wilkes.

"What else?"

James Wilkes shrugged. "Noisy."

"What *else*?"

"Hungry."

James Wilkes wasn't nearly as interested in babies as Iggy. James Wilkes wanted to play football. James Wilkes always wants to play football.

"What else?" Iggy said. "Please tell me. It's very important."

"Loud," said James Wilkes. "Smelly and noisy and hungry and *loud*," and then he ran after a ball that bounced just past his feet.

"James Wilkes isn't an expert," Iggy told me. "He doesn't know anything. He doesn't even *care*. How can he not care?"

"Maybe he does," I said. "Maybe he's just had enough of babies right now."

Iggy shrugged her shoulders high with disbelief. "How is that even *possible?*"

At home, all Iggy could think about and talk about was babies.

"*Pleeease* have one more," she begged. "Just *one.*"

"I'm too old," said Mum.

"Are you?" I said.

"Actually, no," Mum said. "Not exactly. I'm too tired."

Dad nodded. "Babies are exhausting. They are *a lot* of work."

"We'll help you," Iggy said.

"Not enough," said Dad.

"Oh please," Iggy said. "Just. One. Tiny. Baby," and she put her hands a bit apart to show just how tiny it might be.

"Sorry." Mum shook her head. "Just thinking about it is making me tired."

Iggy put her arms out from her sides, like a teapot with two spouts. She said, "What's so exhausting about a *weeny* little baby?"

"Babies keep you awake at night," Mum said. "They are very demanding."

"Babies get cross about nothing for hours at a time," Dad said.

"They need constant care and attention."

"They are always shouting and they are

always pooing and they are always hungry."

"You two sound like James Wilkes," Iggy said.

"Who's that?" Dad asked.

"An expert on babies," I told him.

Iggy glared at all of us.

"Iggy we are *not* having another baby," Mum and Dad told her, at the same time. "*Absolutely* not."

The next week after school, we were having milk and biscuits, and Mum said, "I saw Mrs Wilkes on the high street today."

Iggy had been jabbering away like normal, swinging her legs and talking at a hundred

miles an hour about crayons and guinea pigs and skipping, but suddenly she went a bit quiet.

"Did you?" I said.

"Yes," Mum said. "And we had a nice chat."

Iggy slipped down lower in her chair and her legs stopped swinging.

"What about?" I asked Mum.

"Oh, this and that."

I took a big gulp of milk. Iggy was holding her breath. I could hear her not breathing.

"We talked about babies," Mum said.

"That's nice," I said.

"Mrs Wilkes wanted to know where *my* baby was."

Iggy's eyes were perfect round circles and her mouth was a silent straight line.

"*What* baby?" I asked Mum.

"That's what *I* said."

Iggy made a little groaning noise. It just squeezed out of her. Her cheeks went very pink and she stared very hard at her biscuit.

"Mrs Wilkes was talking about the baby I had last week," Mum said, looking straight at Iggy. "A baby girl called Clover. She was very keen to meet her."

It was ever so quiet at the table after that.

It was too quiet for me to crunch my biscuit. I had to suck it.

"Iggy," Mum said in the end. "Did you make up a baby?"

Iggy shook her head. She kept her lips tight shut.

Mum said, "Think very hard before you answer me, young lady."

Iggy thought very hard. We could see her thinking.

"One lie is bad enough," Mum told her. "Another one won't make it any better."

Iggy's eyebrows went pink, like they always do when she is about to cry. Her chin started to tremble.

"No tears," Mum said. "Tears won't get

you out of trouble either."

"I didn't mean to say it." Iggy still wasn't looking at Mum.

"But you did," Mum told her.

"I couldn't help it," Iggy said.

"Yes you could," Mum said.

"I just pretended," said Iggy. "I just told James Wilkes."

"When?" I asked.

"At playtime," Iggy said.

"And James Wilkes told his mum," Mum said. "And she told me."

Iggy looked at the floor.

"No more pretend babies, Iggy," Mum said.

"OK."

"Just you and Flo and me and Dad."

"OK," Iggy said.

"Sorry?" Mum said.

"Sorry." Iggy nodded.

And nobody said another word about it.

Except when Dad kissed us good night and turned out the lights, he said, "Good night, Flo. Sleep tight, Iggy." And then I heard him whisper, "Good night, Clover."

Iggy's New Teacher

Iggy's teacher was leaving at the end of term and Iggy was extremely upset about it. Rwaida had always been her teacher, since the very first day Iggy started school.

Iggy was really going to miss her.

"I love her," she sobbed, after her last day in Rwaida's class. "I love her and I know where everything is."

"Why does she have to go?" Iggy said. "Why? *Why?*" and she scrunched her hands together into one little fist.

Mum said, "You know Rwaida isn't leaving forever. She's just taking some time off for a happy reason. She will most probably come back."

"Well, *when* will she be back?"

"When she has adopted her baby," said Mum.

"She told us that," Iggy said, "but I don't know what it means."

"Sometimes there are more children than there are families and everybody has to share," I said.

Iggy frowned at me for a minute. She asked Mum, "Is that right?"

"Sort of. Some children don't have families and some families have room for more children."

I said, "Adopting is looking after a baby that you didn't make."

"You don't have to grow it in your tummy?" asked Iggy.

"No," said Mum. "And it's not only babies that can be adopted. Children of all ages need families to take care of them."

"*This* family has got room for more children," said Iggy, spreading her arms as wide as they would go and turning round in a circle. "Can we adopt some?"

Mum shook her head. "I doubt it."

"It wouldn't have to be a baby," Iggy said. "Just somebody smaller than me."

"Wanting to be bigger than someone is not a good reason to adopt," said Mum.

"Well, what is?" asked Iggy.

"Not having children of your own," Mum said. "Or wanting to help others."

"I like helping others," Iggy said, still turning. "I am very good at that."

"Yes you are," said Mum. "And so is Rwaida. She has waited a long time for this baby."

"I know how she feels," said Iggy.

Later, at bathtime, Iggy said, "What will Rwaida do with her baby when she comes back to be my teacher?"

"What baby?" said Dad.

"The baby she is *adopting*," Iggy told him, lying back in the bath with only her face showing through all the bubbles.

"Someone will look after her baby," said Mum. "Someone in Rwaida's family maybe, or a friend, or a childminder."

Iggy sat up with a slosh and Mum poured some shampoo into her hands.

"Can I look after it?" Iggy said, screwing her eyes tight shut to keep out the shampoo.

"I'm very careful. I was very careful with Gruffles."

"Gruffles was a *hamster*," I said, with my mouth full of toothbrush.

"So?" Iggy said. "He was very precious and I didn't break him."

"Babies are a bit different to hamsters." Dad rinsed the bubbles from Iggy's hair. "And anyway, you'll be at school."

"True," said Iggy. She climbed out of the bath and Dad wrapped her in a towel.

Iggy said, "Do you like helping others and taking care of

other people's children?"

"Why?" Dad said. "Is this a trick question?"

"Definitely," said Mum.

Iggy shook her head. "Well, do you?"

Dad looked at me and Mum. "What did I miss?"

Iggy said, "We were thinking about adopting somebody smaller than me."

"No we weren't," said Mum.

"We were *talking* about it," Iggy said.

"*You* were talking about it," Mum said. "We were talking about *Rwaida* adopting somebody smaller than you. That's what *we* were talking about."

Iggy looked up at Dad. "That's why she won't be my teacher any more."

"Have you met your new teacher yet?" he asked.

Iggy looked glum. "Yes."

I told them his name was Trevor. "But he likes to be called Mr Hawthorne."

"Like a prickly old tree," Iggy said.

"Oh dear," said Dad. "Don't you like Mr Hawthorne?"

Iggy gave Dad a withering look from inside her towel. "I *can't* like him," she said. "He's not Rwaida and he's got a moustache."

"Grandad's got a moustache," Mum said.

"Not a big brown twirly one," said Iggy. "Grandad's moustache is smaller than Mr Hawthorne's. And Grandad doesn't wear cowboy boots."

"Cowboy boots?" Mum and Dad smiled at each other.

"Yes," Iggy said. "He's got a twirly moustache and he plays the guitar and he wears cowboy boots. I *love* Rwaida. I'm *never* going to love Mr Hawthorne."

"I'm not sure I'm loving him either," said Dad.

"He is very different from Rwaida," I said.

"Just wait and see," said Mum.

Dad picked Iggy up in her towel and put her over his shoulder. "Bide your time. Wait for the right moment, and then show him who's boss."

"OK," said Iggy.

"Not helpful," said Mum.

On the way downstairs to the kitchen, Iggy's chin began to wobble and her eyes filled up with tears. "I'm scared to have a teacher who isn't Rwaida."

Mum kissed her on the nose and said, "What are we going to do with you?"

"A biscuit would help," Iggy sniffed.

A biscuit usually does.

At the kitchen table, Iggy blew on her hot milk. "What if Mr Hawthorne doesn't know that it's my turn to wipe the board on a Tuesday? What if he forgets I always collect the register on Fridays? How will he know where everybody sits? What if he tries to *change* stuff? What if he doesn't like me? What if he only picks boys for all the good jobs because he is one?"

"Don't worry, Iggy," I said. "It'll be OK."

"How do you know?"

"Because Mr Hawthorne is actually just as nice as Rwaida, but in different ways."

Iggy shook her head. "I've heard he is very strict and he doesn't let you talk in the line and there is no calling out or going to the loo when you need to."

"Well, then you will have to be quiet in the line and not call out or go to the loo all the time," Dad told her.

"I *know*," Iggy said. "That is *exactly* what

I've been worrying about."

"Mr Hawthorne was my teacher once or twice when my real teacher was away. He is actually a lot nicer than he looks," I told her. "He's very funny really and he's got lots of good reading voices."

"What does that mean?" Iggy said, through her biscuit.

"Well, when he's being a giant, he sounds enormous and when he's being a mouse, he sounds small and furry."

"How does he do that?" Iggy said.

"I don't know. He just does."

Iggy raised her eyebrows and picked the crumbs off the table.

"What else does he do?" she asked.

"He's good at PE," I said. "We played lots of pirate ship games in the hall and quite a bit of rounders."

"I'm not very good at rounders," Iggy said. "I'm better at cutting and sticking and glitter."

"Well, you will *get* good at rounders," Mum said. "And other things that Mr Hawthorne is going to teach you."

"Like what?" Iggy said.

"Like Geography and Science and Maths and History," Mum said.

"*Boy* things," mumbled Iggy.

"No young lady," Mum said. "*Everybody* things. Important things."

"He's really not that bad," I said.

Iggy folded her arms and looked at the ceiling. "We'll see."

On her first day in Mr Hawthorne's class, Iggy did not want to go to school. She groaned and grumbled and burrowed deep into her bed like a mole. Mum had to get her up and help her get dressed and march her down the stairs for breakfast.

"I'm not going," Iggy said. "I don't want to go and I'm not going to like it."

Dad said, "I feel like that some mornings before work, but I still go."

"You're a grown-up."

"And so is Mr Hawthorne," said Dad.

"I wonder what he's thinking now."

"What do you mean?" Iggy asked.

"Maybe he doesn't want to go to school either," said Dad.

"Why not?"

"Maybe he's nervous," said Mum. "Maybe he's worried that nobody is going to like him."

"Maybe," Dad said, "he is scared that nobody in the class is going to give him a fair chance. And that everyone is going to say they only like Rwaida and not him."

"Poor Mr Hawthorne," we all said.

Iggy ate her breakfast double quick and dashed upstairs to clean her teeth.

All day at school, I wondered how Iggy was getting on. At playtime, I looked for her, but she wasn't there. I wondered if Mr Hawthorne had kept her in for talking in the line or calling out or going to the loo at the wrong time.

But I didn't need to worry. At the end of the day, when me and Mum went to Iggy's classroom to meet her, she was cleaning the board. And she was smiling.

"Mr Hawthorne put me in charge of *pencils*," she said. "They all have to be sharp and every table has to have all the right colours."

"It's a *desperately* important job," said Mr Hawthorne, and he winked at me and

Mum, and his moustache wiggled.

"Excellent," said Mum. "So you all had a good first day?"

"Lovely," said Iggy, and she smiled again.

"And there was no need for Mr Hawthorne to stay in bed and be so nervous and worried. No need at all."

Iggy's Weekend News

Every Monday, Iggy's new teacher, Mr Hawthorne, asks the children to tell the class their weekend news. Iggy says that sometimes this is interesting, like when Naima Singh went to Italy and ate a pizza, or when Iris Eliot got a rabbit that was bigger than her baby sister, or when Lily Derrick won a trip to the funfair, and sometimes it is not, like when Jade Robinson got stuck in a lift.

According to Iggy, some people in her class get so worked up about having interesting news that they just make it up.

"Last Monday," she told me, "Bailey Grey said he saw a real live dinosaur, but we all know he just went to the park and played football."

"And some people," she said, "called Finn Green, put their hand up every week just to say they haven't got any news at all."

Iggy rolled her eyes very slowly towards the ceiling, which is her new way of showing that she doesn't approve.

Dad said, "Have you got something in your eye?" And Iggy did it again to show that she didn't approve of him either.

Because she knows she has to come up with something to impress Mr Hawthorne on a Monday, and because she doesn't want to make something up, Iggy is very keen to do unusual and fascinating things at the weekend.

At breakfast on Saturday, she rubbed her hands together and made some suggestions.

"Shall we swim with dolphins today?" she said, swirling her spoon in her cornflakes casually. "Or shall we visit Mrs Wilkes and her new baby, or shall we go to Paris and

have a picnic at the top of the Eiffel Tower?"

Dad said something about mowing the lawn and falling asleep under a tree with the radio on. Iggy put her head in her hands. This was not the earth-shattering, jaw-dropping news that she was hoping for.

But Mum had a better idea. She said, "I have found something extremely exciting for *all* of us to do, not too far away."

"*All* of us?" said Dad.

"What is it and when can we go?" said Iggy.

"We can go when you've finished your breakfast and brushed your teeth and hair and put on some scruffy clothes. And you'll see what it is when we get there."

"Do I have to brush my hair?" said Dad, and Iggy sniggered.

We put on our oldest and shabbiest trousers and jumpers.

"Why are we wearing these?" Iggy said.

"Because we'll need them," Mum told her.

"Sounds ominous," said Dad.

"What's 'ominous'?" asked Iggy.

"Scary and worrying," Dad said.

I asked Mum if we were doing anything scary or worrying. I didn't like the sound of that.

"No," she said, and she looked at Dad the way she looks at Iggy when she wants her to behave.

Iggy stuffed her old trousers into her wellington boots. She was all creased and crumpled. We looked at our reflections in the big hall mirror. Dad's shirt was the one he does building things in, covered in paint and bits of sticky stuff. Mum was wearing a grey and baggy old sweatshirt. The sleeves of my jumper were a bit holey and much too short. We all looked very scruffy indeed.

"Perfect," said Mum.

"What a smart and elegant family," Dad said. "I wonder who they are."

Iggy giggled.

"Right," Mum said. "Off we go." She ruffled Iggy's half-brushed hair. "Let's try and take your mind off babies for five minutes."

"We'll see about that," said Iggy.

We went in the car and it only took ten minutes, or three of Iggy's songs.

"Here we are!" Mum said.

"Where?" Iggy and me said together, while we all got out of the car. It didn't look like anywhere to us.

"Through that door." Mum pointed down an alleyway to an old wooden door in the wall.

Iggy looked at me and I looked at the door. It looked ominous.

"Go on," Mum said to us. "Be brave. Go and open it."

Iggy held my hand. We walked up to the door together. Behind us, Dad chattered his teeth and knocked his knees together, as if he was frightened.

"Stop it," said Mum.

"I c-c-c-can't," said Dad.

"What do you think it is?" Iggy asked, out of the side of her mouth.

"I have no idea," I said, out of the side of mine.

"Is it a haunted house?" Iggy's eyes were big and round and scared.

"I don't think so," I told her, but a bit of me did.

The door was dark and heavy and stuck. We pushed it with our hands and feet, and it swung open with a haunted-house groan.

Iggy and me shut our eyes tight and then opened them just a peep.

It wasn't a haunted house at all.

It was a big surprise.

We saw a cobbled yard covered with mud
and straw. We saw stables and sheds. A line
of ducks and ducklings waddled to have a
splash in a muddy puddle. It was smelly and
friendly and noisy. It was a farm. A secret,
hidden, real farm, only ten minutes away
from our house.

Iggy followed the ducklings
to the puddle. They bumped
against her wellington
boots and hopped and
splashed. She crouched
down and counted
them, one by
one.

"How do you

do, Mrs Duck?" she said. "I like your seven ducklings."

Mum smiled. "Happy?"

Iggy nodded, rooted to the spot with delight.

A man came out of a tumbledown barn carrying two full buckets. He smiled at us and we smiled back. He put the buckets down and something slopped and splashed on to the cobbled yard. I could see potato peelings and cabbage leaves and carrot tops in there.

"Lunchtime," said Dad. "Eat up, girls."

The man laughed.

"Hello," he said to Iggy and me. "Who are you?"

"I'm Flo and this is Iggy."

Iggy giggled and hid a little bit behind me.

"I'm Peter," the man said. "I work here. Welcome to the City Farm."

Iggy shuffled and peeked out at Peter. "Are you a farmer?"

Peter nodded.

"He doesn't look like a farmer," she said, in a too-loud whisper.

"What do farmers look like?" Peter said.

Iggy was holding very tightly to the back of my jumper.

"Old and round and muddy with appley cheeks."

Peter laughed again. He was young, quite

tidy, thin and he was wearing jeans. "Well, if I'm not a real farmer, you won't want to help me feed the pigs."

"Yes we will," Iggy said, and she came right out from behind me and tried to lift one of the buckets. It was much too heavy.

"Pigs eat *a lot*," she said.

Peter said, "Pigs are the dustbins of the farmyard," and Iggy giggled.

"The friendliest dustbins in the world," he said, and Iggy snorted.

"Oh," said Peter. "You speak piglet," and Iggy snorted again. "That will come in very handy."

I held Dad's hand and Iggy held Mum's, and we walked with Peter and his buckets to a shed in the far corner of the yard. It was dark in there and smelly, and there was a lot of snorting and squealing and snuffling about.

Iggy saw them first. "Babies!" Iggy hugged herself. "Flo! Look! *Babies!*"

Mum and Dad looked at each other and sighed. I think I counted eleven tiny little piglets. They were squirming and trembly, and they were feeding from their mum, who was lying on her side in the warm stinky straw.

"That's Marmalade," Peter said. "Poor girl. She's a bit worn out."

We watched as Peter went in through the gate and poured the buckets into

Marmalade's trough. She looked up at him and made a grunting noise, and then slowly and carefully she got up to have her lunch. The tiny piglets rolled and squealed and tumbled over each other in the straw.

Iggy cooed and sighed. She tried to speak piglet.

"Would you like to hold one?" Peter asked us.

Iggy jumped up and down on the spot.

"Yes please," I said.

Peter picked up two tiny pink piglets. Iggy cradled hers just like a baby and I stroked mine. It was soft and warm and wriggly.

"Oh, Flo, look," Iggy said. "Look at his *eyelashes*," and she groaned with joy.

My piglet blinked up at me with its dark eyes. Iggy tickled her piglet's tummy and gave it a little kiss.

"Can we live here?" Iggy asked.

"Well," Mum said. "We live ten minutes away."

"I want to live *here*," Iggy said.

"Are you sensible?" Peter asked, and Iggy pulled her most sensible face, which is very staring and serious.

"I think we are," I said.

"Oh good." Peter took the piglets and put them back with their mum. "We need sensible people who live ten minutes away to come here and do lots of helping."

"What sort of helping?" I said.

"Well, we need to bottle-feed a couple of the lambs," said Peter.

"Lambs? *Where?*" Iggy interrupted.

"In the field at the back," he said, "next to the goats."

"Goats?"

"And the donkeys need brushing and feeding and watering," said Peter.

I love donkeys. They are my favourite animals ever.

"Can we help?" I asked Mum and Dad. "Can we come after school and at the weekends and help?"

"Of course you can," Mum and Dad and Peter said, at the same time.

"And there's Ermentrude," Peter said. "She's my favourite."

"Who's Ermentrude?" Iggy asked.

"She's the new calf. She was born three weeks ago. Would you like to see her? Oh, and the rabbits and kittens," he said, smiling. "I almost forgot the new rabbits and kittens. They've just been born."

Iggy looked at Mum and Dad. "See?" she said. "*Everyone's* having babies."

"Yes," Peter said, "it's that time of year."

Iggy stuffed her hands in her pockets. "Not in our house."

We followed Peter across the cobbled

yard, away from the piglets.

"Piglets and rabbits and kittens and lambs and calves and donkeys and ducklings and chicks and piglets and rabbits and..." Iggy chanted, while she skipped and sploshed through the mud and the straw and the puddles. "Just *wait* until I tell Mr Hawthorne my weekend news on Monday. It's going to be the best *ever*."

The Measuring Door

For a long time, Iggy was the smallest person in her class. This meant that she was actually the smallest person in our whole school.

This was not Iggy's favourite thing to be. She wanted very much to grow. She was feeling quite impatient about growing.

Mum and Dad tried to reassure her. They said that growing was a thing that Iggy and me were both really good at.

"Flo's better at it than me," Iggy said, and she showed us all how she only almost came up to my shoulder.

"I've been doing it longer," I told her. "I've had a head start."

Mum said, "You are both doing it all the time."

Dad said, "You are even doing it in your sleep."

"How is that possible?" Iggy asked. "The only thing you are doing in your sleep is dreaming."

Mum and Dad told Iggy that wasn't true.

"A sleeping person can be doing all kinds of things," said Mum.

"Like what?" she asked.

"Like twitching," Dad said, "and rolling about, and talking nonsense."

"And snoring," said Mum.

"And *growing*?" Iggy said.

Dad nodded.

According to Mum and Dad, when you are asleep, you are doing all the stuff that you didn't have time for in the day when you were awake.

"You are putting all the things you have seen and done and learned into the right boxes in your brain, so that in the morning you can wake up and start again," said Dad.

I had no idea how busy a sleeping person could be.

Iggy had no idea there were any boxes in her brain. "How did they get in there? What happens when they are full?"

"They're not *real* boxes," Mum said. "They're just spaces for information. And they can never get full, because the more you put in them the bigger they grow."

"Unlike *me*," Iggy said.

Usually when I see Iggy at playtime, she is running about like a pony, and skipping and squealing and hula-hooping. She is always with her gang of friends, like a flock of noisy birds darting from one corner of the playground to the other. But today, she was hanging from the monkey bars by herself, doing nothing. She wasn't swinging or laughing or even moving at all. She was just dangling like a wet shirt on a washing line.

It was strange seeing Iggy so still and on her own. I went to talk to her.

"Are you OK?" I asked.

"Yep," she said, and she carried on dangling. Her arms were very straight and her face was very red.

"Where are your friends?" I said. "Why aren't you playing?"

Iggy stretched out her legs and looked down at her shoes.

"I'm too busy," she said.

"Busy doing what?"

Iggy looked at me as if the answer was perfectly obvious.

"I am *growing*."

Her hands were gripping very tightly to the bars. Her arms must have been aching. It looked like hard work.

Iggy stared up at her hands and puffed out her cheeks. "I think I can feel it working."

I asked Iggy how long she was going to hang there for, not running or skipping or squealing or hula-hooping or darting about.

Iggy sighed. "As long as it takes."

At home, Mum and Dad asked me how my day had been. They asked me how Iggy's day had been. I was just going to tell them about the monkey bars, when Iggy came into the room with two very big and heavy-looking bags. She was huffing and puffing with the effort of carrying them, but she didn't put them down.

"What have you got in there?" Dad said.

Iggy looked down at the bags and blew her fringe out of her eyes. "Books."

"What books?" said Mum.

"My books," said Iggy.

"What are you doing with them?"

"Growing my arms."

Mum and Dad looked at each other.

Dad's face said, "Can I laugh?" and Mum's face said, "NO."

I asked Iggy if it was harder or easier than hanging from the monkey bars all playtime. She tried to shrug, but the bags were too heavy. She couldn't move her shoulders.

"About the same," she said.

"Why do you only want to grow your arms?" Dad asked.

"I don't," Iggy said. "I want to grow the rest of me as well. I'm just starting with my arms."

"Then what?" said Dad. "Shall we make you some extremely heavy shoes from bricks, to grow your legs?"

"OK," said Iggy.

"Or better still, you could have a bath and then we could wring you out like a jumper.

Mum's good at making all my jumpers really big when she washes them."

"Good idea!" Iggy said, and she dropped her books on the floor with a loud thud. "Can I have a bath now?"

"No," said Mum. "I wouldn't risk that. I'm good at shrinking jumpers too."

Iggy shuddered. She definitely was not interested in getting any smaller. She sighed and slumped into a chair. She looked around the kitchen. She was exasperated.

"When am I *ever* going to grow?" she said. "*Everyone* is taller than me."

"You *will* grow," Mum said. "You'll be as tall as me one day, maybe taller. You are doing all the right things."

"Like hanging from monkey bars and carrying books?" Iggy said.

"No, like eating and drinking good things, and running and swimming."

"And sleeping," I said. "Don't forget sleeping."

"I won't," Iggy said. "I'm going to go and do some of that right now."

Iggy had *never* gone to bed without being told before. Not once. Usually she makes lots of excuses why she shouldn't, and has lots of reasons to stay up for five more minutes.

Mum and Dad looked at each other.

Mum said, "That's not like you," and Dad said, "Is this a trick?"

"It's not a trick. I just want to do some

growing, that's all," Iggy said, and she dragged her heavy bags of books up the stairs to bed.

"Oh dear," said Dad.

"Poor thing," said Mum. "It's hard being small."

In the morning, while we were eating our cornflakes, Mum said something that surprised us. "Hurry up and eat your breakfast. We are going to let you draw on the wall."

I stopped crunching. Iggy swallowed, and her mouth closed up tight and she frowned up at Mum.

"No you're not," she said. "You never let us draw on the wall. It is *absolutely* forbidden."

"Quite true. But today we are making an exception."

"What's one of those?" Iggy asked, and I told her it's when a grown-up changes their mind.

"OK," said Iggy. "What are we drawing? Can we draw anything we like?"

"No," Mum said. "We are drawing a height chart."

"What for?"

"We are going to measure ourselves and make marks on the doorframe to show how tall we are."

Iggy shook her head. "No thanks. I don't want to. I already know how tall I am and it's not very."

"You know how tall you are *now*," Mum said. "But you don't know how tall you will be in one month's time. We can measure you again then, and compare."

"I will probably be exactly the same," Iggy said, "because I am not growing."

Mum got a pen. "Well, let's make a mark on the doorframe and see."

And that is just what we did. We had to stand very straight and still while Mum and Dad made a mark. Next to the mark, we wrote down our name and the date. We measured everyone. Dad was at the top, then Mum, then a big gap, then me, then Iggy.

"See?" she said, not smiling. "I'm still the

smallest. I'm always the smallest," and she
stomped up the stairs to brush her teeth.

"Oh dear," Mum said. "The measuring
door didn't quite work."

At playtime, Iggy still wasn't running about like a pony, or skipping and squealing and hula-hooping with her friends. She was alone again, hanging from the monkey bars. She was upside down this time, with all her hair falling towards the ground. Her face was as red as a beetroot, and she looked very glum.

She looked glum on the way home too. When we got there, instead of playing in the garden with me or rooting about in the kitchen for biscuits, Iggy went straight to her bedroom on her own. Iggy doesn't often go anywhere on her own. She is usually very fond of company.

One thing Iggy likes to do on her own is play schools. She takes the register and she gives homework and there is no misbehaving in her class. I think she likes it because she gets to be the boss of everyone. She says, 'Stop fidgeting, Polly. And, Mumble, I'm very disappointed. Your handwriting is usually much better than that.'

I remembered this as I sat in the kitchen and looked at the marks we had made that morning. I hoped Iggy was playing schools in her room with all her teddies. Suddenly I knew how to make Iggy feel better.

I ran upstairs and knocked on her door.

"Come in," she said, in a glum voice. She

wasn't playing anything. She was sitting on her bed.

"Sorry to disturb you," I said, "but I've just remembered something about the measuring door."

Iggy sighed and looked at the carpet. "I don't want to talk about that."

"But we haven't measured everyone yet."

"What do you mean?"

I picked up some of Iggy's best teddies.

"Will you help?" I asked her.

We took them into the kitchen, to the measuring door. We started to measure them.

"Keep still, Mumble," I said. "No wriggling."

Iggy stopped frowning.

We made little marks and wrote down the teddies' names and the date, just like we had done with Mum and Dad.

When we had finished, we stepped back to have a look.

"See? You're not the smallest," I said to Iggy. "You are much, much taller than Mumble and Polly and Ranger."

"True," Iggy said, stretching a bit.

"And you are a *giant* compared to Hunter and Gloria."

"I am, aren't I? I am actually very tall in toy world."

We looked at the height chart that we had made. Iggy wasn't the smallest any more.

"Thanks, Flo," Iggy said.

"That's OK," I said, and I put my arm around her. She stood on tiptoes and she nearly almost rested her head on my shoulder.

The School Fair

Most of the time, Iggy comes out of her classroom with a hop and a skip and a smile. She talks at a hundred miles an hour and she nearly always has good news to tell us on the way home.

But the other day, Iggy came out of her classroom with a face like thunder. She stomped over to where I was waiting for Dad, and with every stomp her frown got darker and her bottom lip stuck out further.

"What's the matter with you?" I said. I thought maybe somebody else's mum was having a baby.

Iggy stopped stomping and folded her arms high across her chest. Her cheeks were flushed pink with fury. She took a deep breath in.

"Frankie Day and Ella James and Louis Green and Marouane Saddowi and Jacob Warner *all* got a special letter to take home, and *I* didn't get one."

"Why didn't you get one?" I asked.

"Because we're *saving paper*," Iggy said,

and she put her arms out like the branches of a tree and rolled her eyes, as if saving paper was the craziest idea she'd ever heard.

"That's good," I told her. "Saving paper is a good thing. Saving paper saves trees. You know that."

At home, we are only allowed to draw on the back of Mum's used work paper, and we make a lot of things out of old magazines. This is called recycling.

Iggy nodded. "Yes I know about saving trees. But what I *don't* know," she said, through gritted teeth, "is what was in that letter."

Iggy hates not knowing things when other people do. Nothing makes her madder than not being in on a secret.

"Well, that's easy," I said. "It's about the School Fair. You didn't get a letter, because I did. The people in your class who got a letter are the ones without big brothers and sisters. You didn't get one, because you can read mine."

Iggy's frown lifted a bit. She un-gritted her teeth. Her hands turned into pincers, like a little lobster or a crab.

"Can I read it now?" she said, and her pincers opened and shut double quick while I looked for it in my bag.

When I gave her the letter, Iggy clasped it with both hands. There were too many words in it for her to read all at once, but she looked it over and then hugged it to her chest and smiled.

"I love the School Fair," she said.

I love the School Fair too. Everyone's at school, but it's not a school day. There is more laughing and running about than normal, and more food and colour and noise, and much less getting told off. Everything's the same and everything's different.

When Dad collected us, Iggy waved the letter at him, right up close so it tickled his nose.

"The School Fair is coming!"

Dad lifted Iggy and the letter up on to

his shoulders. "Great," he said. "The School Fair again." But he didn't sound even half as happy as we were.

Iggy beamed from up high. "It *is* great. It is very exciting." She waved the letter in the air like a flag.

Dad walks very fast, because of his long legs. I had to skip every fifth step to keep up.

"Tell me why it's exciting," Dad said. "Tell me exactly why."

So we did.

"The whole playground gets *transformed*," Iggy said "As if by *magic*," and she forgot to hold on to Dad's head while she made a magic spell in the sky.

"It's always fun and there's something for everyone," I said.

"There's a cake stall. And a book stall. You like books."

"There's face painting," Iggy said. "And crazy hair colours."

"And a fancy-dress parade. This year the theme is The World."

"Well," said Dad. "That narrows it down a bit."

"There's throwing wet sponges at teachers," I said.

"Oh, now I do like that," said Dad.

"Me too." Iggy covered her face with the letter and peeped out. "It's very *naughty.*"

"There's a climbing wall," I said.

The climbing wall is my favourite. Last year, I got to the very top. When I looked around me, I could see the whole fair down below. I could see my friends eating ice cream and playing skittles. I could see the canal behind the playground, and the cars on the road, and the school roof with all the footballs and things that get lost on it.

"I couldn't go on the climbing wall," Iggy grumbled. "I wasn't allowed because I was too small."

"But you are growing," I said, "and it was a whole year ago."

Iggy looked down at us. "Oh yes! I have. I've grown loads. I'm taller than Dad, see?"

"Then you're definitely tall enough," Dad told her.

Iggy squinted at the letter. "There's a raffle, but I don't know what that is. It sounds silly."

"It's not silly," I told her. "It's got really good prizes."

"Can I win a wet weekend in February?" asked Dad.

"No," I said. "But I think there's a meal for two."

When we got home, we still weren't tired of talking about the fair. Mum made us some toast, and Iggy read the whole letter out loud. I helped her with the difficult bits. It was full of important information about the things we needed to make and do.

"For the first time," Iggy read, "there will be an art com-pet-it-ion, with two cat-eg-or-ies – a garden on a plate and a self-portrait."

Iggy stopped reading. "Why would you

put a garden on a plate?"

Nobody said anything, because nobody knew why.

I said, "I'm going to do a self-portrait."

"Me too." Iggy nodded. "I'm going to do mine with pasta."

Nobody said anything to that either.

I thought about doing my self-portrait. To make one of those, you have to look in the mirror for a long time. It is a funny feeling, like having a staring competition with yourself, and nobody wins.

Iggy thought about what costume to wear for the fancy-dress parade. Dressing up is one of Iggy's favourite things ever. First she said she would go as the Sahara Desert, then as an Indian lady in a sari, and finally as an Egyptian Pyramid.

"We can make me out of a cardboard box," she said. "It'll be easy."

"I could go as the Sphinx," I said.

"Good idea, Flo," said Dad. "Me and Mum will dress up as a camel."

Iggy sniggered.

"Will we?" said Mum. "I don't think so."

"But will you be a volunteer?" I asked. "The letter says we need lots of those."

"What's a volunteer?" asked Iggy.

"It's someone who does something out of the goodness of their own heart," Dad said.

Iggy smiled. "I like the sound of that."

On the day of the fair, we got up early and iced sixty cupcakes. Iggy put on her cardboard Pyramid costume. I put on my Sphinx headdress, and Mum painted our faces so we looked as if we were made out of stone. The walk to school took

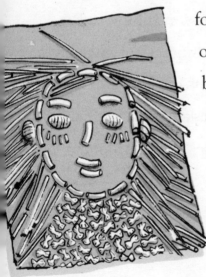

forever, because Iggy could only take tiny steps in her box. She carried her pasta self-portrait and I carried my painted one. Mum carried the cupcakes and Dad carried three boxes of books.

When we got there, the playground *had* been transformed. The tables from our classrooms were all outside, piled high with things and prizes. There was a white tent filled with all the gardens on plates and the portraits for the art competition.

Iggy bought a one-eared rabbit from the toy stall, and six tickets for the raffle. I bought a book about dolphins, and a bracelet.

Suddenly Iggy came running towards me out of the crowds. "Quick," she said. "We need to get Dad."

"What for?"

"Mr Hawthorne is looking for a volunteer."

We found Dad and told him.

"I told Mr Hawthorne you would do it," Iggy said.

Dad looked worried. "Do what?"

Iggy shrugged. "I don't know."

We pulled Dad by the hands over to where Mr Hawthorne was waiting. It was the throw-a-wet-sponge-at-the-teacher stall.

"Oh no," said Dad.

"Oh yes," said Mr Hawthorne.

There was a big queue of people ready to throw sponges, and nobody to throw them at.

Mr Hawthorne was dripping wet. "All the teachers are soaked. It's throw-a-wet-sponge-at-the-parent now."

Dad looked up at the sky. "What have I done to deserve this?" he said, and he took his coat off.

"You've *volunteered*," Iggy told him, and she clapped her hands together with excitement and delight.

Dad bent down. He put his arms through the armholes and his head through the headhole of the throw-a-wet-sponge stall.

"Ready?" asked Mr Hawthorne.

Dad tried to nod.

"Steady?"

And before anyone could say, "GO!" a big fat dripping-wet sponge flew through the air and landed on Dad's head, sliding down his nose and hitting the ground with a splosh.

"OOF!" said Dad. His hair was all plastered down. He tried to blow the water off his face, the way Iggy blows on her fringe. He was blinking furiously.

Iggy and me jumped up and down and hid
our eyes.

"Mum!" we shouted. "Mum! Come and
see this!"

The next wet sponge was already on its way.

"AWF!" said Dad. The water ran down his neck and inside his shirt and made him wriggle.

Mum arrived just in time to see the third sponge land, and the fourth and the fifth and sixth. She thought it was the funniest thing she had seen all day. Even after Mr Hawthorne had let Dad go, and he'd dried himself a bit on a towel and had a hot cup of tea, Mum was still laughing.

Iggy asked me to take her to the climbing wall. We left her cardboard-box Pyramid with Mum at the cake stall. We crossed our fingers behind our backs while the man measured her, and we held our breaths.

"On you go," he said, with a smile, as he helped us into our harnesses.

"Am I tall enough?" Iggy asked him.

"Just about."

Iggy beamed. She punched the air. She did a little dance, until the man told her to stay still while he tightened the straps.

"I've grown," she told him. "I've grown quite a lot."

Then Iggy and me went together to the top of the climbing wall. I showed her the canal and the cars and the stuff on the school roof. We looked down at the whole noisy, colourful, fluttering, perfect fair, with Dad helping Mum sell cupcakes, and our friends running about flying miniature kites.

"Wow, Flo," said Iggy, skinny and scruffy without her cardboard box, and grinning from ear to ear. "*Wow*."

And we waved.

Twenty Questions

Iggy and me were lounging about, watching TV and feeling a bit bored. Mum was on the phone. Suddenly we heard a noise. It was a shouty, excited noise. It wasn't coming from the TV. Then Mum danced past the door, hopping up and down in the hall. The noise was coming from Mum.

"What's happened?" we asked, but Mum didn't tell us.

She spoke into the phone.

"Got to go now, bye!"

"Who was that?" we said.

Mum smiled. "Nobody."

Iggy pointed her finger at Mum. "You can't talk on the phone to *Nobody*."

Mum's smile got bigger. "True. It was somebody."

"Who?"

"Somebody with some *very* exciting news."

Iggy loves news, but if she can't find it out in an instant, she gets all tense and tightly coiled, like a spring.

She shot forward in her seat. "What is it?"

Her forehead was crinkled with questions.

I wanted to know too.

Mum smiled an especially big smile, but she still wouldn't tell us.

"You'll have to wait until Dad gets home."

"I don't like waiting," Iggy said, banging her shoe against the wall. "I'm not very good at waiting at all."

"If you practise waiting," said Mum, "you will get better at it."

"I don't think I want to get better at it," Iggy said. "I think I just want to know *now*."

Iggy sighed as loud as she could sigh. She banged her shoe against the wall and Mum asked her to stop. Then she started picking at the wallpaper and Mum asked her to stop that too.

"Stop hanging about sighing and banging and picking at things," said Mum. "Go and do something."

"Like what?"

"Draw a picture, put your roller skates on, watch some more telly, go outside and throw a tennis ball against the wall."

"I *can't* do anything until I know the extra special and exciting news," Iggy said.

This is how Iggy gets to know a thing, by refusing to do anything else until you tell her. Dad says this technique is very effective. He says it can wear a person down.

But Mum wasn't being worn down.

"*Out*," she said. "Go and run twenty times around the garden."

"And then will you tell me?" said Iggy.

Mum said she would think about it.

Iggy said, "And so will I."

"Is it really, *really* special and exciting news?" I asked, when Iggy had gone. "Will we be delighted?"

"I think you will," said Mum. "I think we all will."

Iggy didn't run around the garden twenty times. She walked around it twice and then she came back in, more desperate to know than ever.

"Are we getting a dog?" she said.

"No."

"A cat?"

"A budgerigar?"

"Are we going on holiday?"

"No."

"Did we win something? Did *I* win something?"

"No and No."

"I can't *bear* it," Iggy said, like the ladies

in the black-and-white films that Granny watches.

"Oh dear," said Mum. "That's a shame."

Iggy flopped into a chair and did some more sighing. She drummed her hands on the table. She drummed them fast and loud.

"Please don't do that," said Mum.

"If I stop," said Iggy, "will you tell me?"

"If you stop," said Mum, "I won't send you to your room on your own."

Iggy stopped straightaway. Iggy is not a fan of being alone.

Just then, Dad walked in.

"He's here!" said Iggy, shooting out of her chair. "Tell us the news!"

"What news?" Dad said. "Is there news?"

"Yes!" said Iggy, holding on to herself like she might be about to take off. "There is extra special and exciting news and we have been waiting all day for you to come home so we can know it."

"Half an hour actually," said Mum.

"Well," said Iggy. "It felt longer."

"Well, go on then," said Dad, sitting down at the table and ruffling up my hair. "Tell us."

Mum smiled at Dad and Iggy and Me. "I have a big surprise for you," she said.

Iggy sat with her chin on her knees. She couldn't be folded up any tighter.

"What's the big surprise about?" I asked.

"Not what," Mum said, "but who."

"Well, who then?" asked Iggy, and she started banging her shoe against the leg of her chair.

Mum said, "Stop banging please, Iggy," and Iggy said, "Only. When. I. Know."

Mum and Dad looked at each other.

"Let's play Twenty Questions," Dad said, and Iggy groaned.

Twenty Questions is a game we play on long journeys when we have run out of snacks and other things to do. You think of a person, and everyone else has twenty questions to work out who the person is. They are supposed to be the sort of questions you can only say 'yes' or 'no' to. Sometimes this can be quite tricky.

"Let's play," Mum said, "and then you can work out what the big surprise is for yourself."

"Who is it?" Iggy said, one more time.

You are not allowed to ask, "Who is it?" in Twenty Questions. If you were, it would be called One Question and it wouldn't be much fun at all.

"Nineteen questions left," said Mum.

"Have we met them before?" I said.

"Yes," said Mum.

"Are they real?" Iggy asked.

"Yes," said Mum, and Dad said, "Who do we know who isn't real?"

"Famous people or something." Iggy shrugged. "I thought it might be a big exciting surprise about somebody famous."

"Famous people are real," Mum said.

"No they're *not*," Iggy said. "Don't be *silly*."

"Seventeen questions," said Mum.

"Is it somebody famous?" Iggy said.

"No sorry, Iggy, they're not famous," Mum said.

"Are they nearby?" I asked.

"No. They are a very long way away," said Mum.

"Ooh," said Iggy. "Are they aliens from another planet?"

"No. They're not aliens."

"Oh. Are they human beings?"

"Yes. They are definitely human beings."

"Not animals or cartoon characters or film stars?"

Mum shook her head. "Human beings," she said. "Ten questions."

"Are they younger than you?" I said.

"Yes," said Mum. "They are younger."

"*Everyone's* younger than us," said Dad.

"Except for Granny and Grandad," Iggy

said, "and Mrs Butler from next door."

"True," said Dad.

"Nine questions," said Mum.

"Are they *funnier* than you?" Iggy said.

Dad gasped in horror and put his hands on his cheeks. "Nobody is funnier than us," he said. "*Nobody.*"

Iggy giggled.

"Are they handsomer than you?" I said, and Dad sighed and slumped his shoulders and gazed forlornly at his reflection in the window.

"Probably," he said.

"Definitely," said Mum, grinning.

"Seven questions," Dad said.

Iggy jumped up and down on the spot and

made a funny nervous noise. She loves it when the questions start running out, because she is getting closer and closer to knowing.

"Do we like them?" she said.

"We like them a lot," Mum said. "We love them."

"*Four* questions," Iggy said, and she rubbed her hands together in anticipation.

"No, Iggy," said Dad. "Six questions. No cheating."

Iggy put her head in her hands. "I just want it to be finished. I just want to know."

Suddenly I thought I knew who it was.

"Oh! Do they live in America?" I said.

"Yes," said Mum.

"Are they in our family?" I asked.

"Yes!"

"Ooh! Ooh!" said Iggy, with her hand up, jiggling about so much that the cups and plates on the shelf were jangling and shaking, like in a little earthquake. "Is it…? Is it Auntie Kate and Uncle Chuck?"

"Yes! You guessed it, Iggy! With three questions to spare!"

Iggy did a little dance. She pitter-pattered her feet on the kitchen floor and she flapped her arms and waggled about.

"Auntie Kate and Uncle Chuck," she sang, while she waggled.

Auntie Kate is Mum's little sister. She is three years younger than Mum, just like Iggy and me. She lives in America. Uncle Chuck

is Auntie Kate's boyfriend. He is from New York. He is very big and tall and he has extremely white teeth. He is a photographer and he has enormous feet. Mum thinks he is very handsome. Dad thinks Chuck is a silly name, but he says when someone is that big and tall you don't tell them.

Iggy and me love Auntie Kate and Uncle Chuck.

"What is their extra special and exciting news?" I said.

Mum's smile was even bigger than Iggy's.

"What's the thing that Iggy wants more than anything else in the world?" she asked.

Iggy gasped and put her hands over her mouth.

"Can you guess?" asked Mum, and Iggy nodded. Her eyes were big and wide and round.

"Auntie Kate and Uncle Chuck are having a *baby!*" Mum said, and she danced about in the kitchen, just like a grown-up Iggy.

And then we all danced. Even Dad. It was the most extra special and exciting news we had ever heard.

A baby.

In the Rabbit Hole

After Mum told us that Auntie Kate and Uncle Chuck were having a baby, we found out three very interesting things.

The first thing we found out was that most babies take a bit more than nine months to grow. A bit more than nine months is forty weeks, or two hundred and eighty days.

Iggy said, "That is so so *so* long to wait," but I thought it was quite a short time for making a human, and Mum and Dad thought so too.

"And anyway," Mum said, "Auntie Kate is already nearly four months pregnant, so there are only five months left to go."

"Which is only twenty weeks," Dad said. "Or one hundred and forty days."

Iggy groaned.

The second thing was that babies don't actually have to be born in a hospital. Some babies are born at home, even in the bath, and some just pop out on the way to the shops or at the hairdressers or in the backs of taxis.

Auntie Kate would like to have her baby

in a birthing pool, which sounds like a bath, only bigger.

When I told Dad, he said, "That sounds like Auntie Kate." He said, "I bet there will be candles."

The third thing we found out was that Mum is an extremely brilliant knitter. As soon as she knew there was a baby coming, she started making things. When she wasn't working, or playing with us, or cooking, or sorting out the airing cupboard, suddenly she was very busy with a bag of wool and two clickety-clackety knitting needles.

The first time we saw Mum knitting, we were on our way past the sitting room. Iggy was in front of me, and I nearly walked

right into her because she suddenly stopped
and pointed to what Mum was up to.

"What's that?" she said.

"It's a shoe," Mum said.

"No it's not," Iggy said. "Shoes aren't made
like that. Shoes are made by shoemakers.
They are made of leather and buckles and
things. Not wool."

"Shoes for babies are made of wool," said
Mum.

Iggy folded her arms. "Shoes made of wool
are *socks*."

"Good point," Mum said. "It's a sock
then," and her needles went clickety-clack.
They were moving so fast they were almost
a blur.

"How do you make socks?" I asked. "Is it hard?"

Mum shook her head, but she kept her eyes on her knitting and she was frowning with concentration. "Not really. Maybe a bit."

"If socks are hard to make," said Iggy, "why don't you just buy some? They are everywhere, in all the shops."

Mum smiled, but she didn't stop knitting. "You sound just like your dad."

The next time we looked, after we had played five games of snakes and ladders, the sock had grown a little bit. And the next time, when we were in the middle of making a den in Iggy's room using all the cushions and sheets and towels, there it was – a sock, perfect and finished on the arm of the sofa. Mum was already making another one.

"What a lovely tiny woolly sock," said Iggy, holding it in her palm.

It was soft and fluffy and the colour of porridge. It looked just the right shape and size for a baby's foot.

"That's very clever," I said to Mum, and Mum said, "Thanks."

"Will you teach us to knit?" I asked her. "I'd like to make something for the baby."

"Ooh, me too," said Iggy, diving into Mum's bag of wool and ferreting about. "But I don't want to make socks. I want to make something special and useful."

"Like what?" Mum said.

"Like a sausage-dog doorstop," Iggy said. "Or a tea cosy. Those are the sorts of things that *I* want to make. You can't buy *them* in the shops."

"But babies don't need sausage dogs or tea cosies," Mum said. "They need socks and hats and jackets and blankets."

"Why?" said Iggy.

"To keep them warm."

Iggy frowned. "Why wouldn't a sausage-dog doorstop keep them warm? Isn't that what it's for?"

"Yes," said Mum, "I suppose it is. But you need to start with something easier."

"Like a tea cosy?"

"Or maybe a scarf. Scarves are always useful and they are a good place to start."

"Do babies wear scarves?" I said.

"Babies might wear a big scarf," Mum said, "like a blanket."

Iggy put the sock back on the arm of the sofa. "Well then, I'll make a big scarf. But does it have to be the colour of porridge?"

"No. What colour do you want it to be?"

"Purple," Iggy said. "And green and blue and orange and red and yellow."

Iggy thinks that babies should wear bright and loud and happy colours because babies are bright and loud and happy.

"I'll see what I've got," said Mum. She rummaged in her bag and found some red wool. "Will this do to start with?"

She patted the sofa either side of her, for us to sit down and watch.

Iggy rubbed her hands together and jiggled in her seat. "Let's *do* it," she said.

Mum picked up a knitting needle and the ball of red wool. She made a loop in the end of the wool and put the needle through it.

Iggy stopped jiggling. She said, "When and how did you do that?"

"Just now," Mum said. "Like this," and she took the needle out of the loop, pulled the wool back into a straight line, and did it all again before we could count to three.

"Wow," said Iggy, staring at Mum and then leaning forward to look over at me.

Mum smiled. "I'll just start it off," and she picked up another needle. Her hands started moving and the needles clicked and clacked together. Soon she had more than twenty loops on the needle, just like the first one.

We were amazed, but all Mum said was, "That's called casting on."

We couldn't believe what we were seeing. Mum was a magician performing tricks.

Iggy's eyebrows were as high as they could go, and she pursed her mouth as if she was about to whistle and then let out a very high-pitched squeak. Iggy thinks that's what whistling is.

"We will *never* be able to do that," I said.

"Oh yes you will," Mum said, and even though she was looking at us, her magic hands knew just what to do and her needles carried on clickety-clacking.

"When I was little," she said, still knitting, "about the same age as Iggy is now, my mum taught me a rhyme."

"What rhyme?" we asked.

"In the rabbit hole, round the tree, out the rabbit hole and off go we," Mum recited.

Iggy scratched her head. "Well, it's a very nice rhyme," she said, "but it's a bit babyish. And I thought we were learning how to knit."

"You are," Mum said. "It's a knitting rhyme. It's a rhyme about knitting."

Iggy looked at me and shrugged. She said, "How can it be about knitting when it's about *rabbits?*"

"Watch," Mum said, and she did exactly what she had been doing, only she did it very, very slowly.

"In the rabbit hole," she said, and she put

one needle into a loop on the other needle.

"Round the tree," and she wrapped the wool around it once.

"Out the rabbit hole," she said, pulling the needle out again and making a new loop.

"And off go we!"

Iggy rubbed her eyes.

"Do it again," I said, and this time we watched extra carefully.

"*In* the rabbit hole." The needle went in.

"*Round* the tree." The wool went round.

Iggy was kneeling on the sofa now to get a better look. She was getting a bit fidgety.

"*Out* the rabbit hole." The needle came out like before.

"And off go we!"

Iggy smacked her forehead into the palm of her hand. "I'm not doing that. I'm going outside to ride my bike. Knitting is too difficult for me."

If Iggy can't do something straightaway, she just gives up. Dad says she will grow out of it.

"You have a go," Mum said to me, and she gave me the needles to hold. They were joined together by the wool. I felt very strange and clumsy, like the time I tried to write my name with my foot instead of my hand.

"In the rabbit hole," Mum said, helping me. "Round the tree. That's it. Out the rabbit hole…"

"…And off go we!" I joined in.

I did it.

Mum helped me, but I did it.

And I did it again. I did it twenty times until I got to the end, and then I turned the needles round and started again.

When Iggy came back from riding her bike, her hair was wild and windy and her cheeks were numb with cold. She put her head round the door of the sitting room where I was knitting. She looked at me like I was a magician now too.

"Wow, Flo," she whispered. "Just Wow."

Later, after supper, Dad was reading the newspaper and Mum was knitting and so was I. Iggy was doing a lot of sighing.

"What's the matter, Iggy?" said Dad.

"I'm a tiny bit bored."

"Do you want a turn?" I said. "Maybe I could help you, now I know how."

Iggy shook her head and scrunched up her nose.

"It's not as hard as it looks," I said.

"Well, it looks *extremely* hard," Iggy said. "And I don't think I can do it."

"Just like riding a bike," Dad said, "and swimming."

"And tying your shoelaces," said Mum, "and plaiting Flo's hair."

Iggy frowned at them. "What do you mean? I can do all of those things. I'm very good at them."

"Exactly," Mum said. "But before you

could do them, they looked hard, and you gave up straightaway."

Iggy folded her arms and sighed again. I patted the sofa next to me, for her to come and watch, and I knitted extra carefully and slowly. Iggy leaned in until her nose was very close to my hands. I knitted a few stitches.

"See?" I said. "In the rabbit hole, round the tree."

"Yes," said Iggy, squeezing herself in front of me, sort of on to my lap, as if we were both riding a bike and my knitting was the handlebars. "I see."

She held on to the needles with me and we did the next bit together.

"Out the rabbit hole. And off go we!"

In the next five months, or twenty weeks, or one hundred and forty days, we got quite good at knitting. We knitted the baby a whole, extra long, rainbow coloured scarf. We took it in turns, just Iggy and me. And when it was finished, we put it in the drawer with all the soft and fluffy porridge-coloured things that Mum had made.

"Our scarf is definitely the brightest and loudest and happiest thing in there," Iggy said. "It's going to be the baby's favourite."

And we waited for the baby to come and wear it.

Iggy and Me and the New Baby

Auntie Kate and Uncle Chuck came to stay with us a few weeks before the baby was supposed to be born. We had to move around in our house to fit them in, like a game of musical beds.

Mum and Dad said that Iggy would have

to move into my room and sleep with me.

"Auntie Kate and Uncle Chuck are never going to fit in my bed," Iggy told them. "They are much too tall and full of baby. They will be very uncomfortable."

"They aren't going to sleep in your room," Mum said. "We are. Auntie Kate and Uncle Chuck are going to sleep in our bed."

"Well, how will *you* fit in my bed?" Iggy asked.

"With great difficulty," said Dad.

"Maybe one of us should sleep on the sofa," Mum said.

"Ooh, I like it," Iggy said, rubbing her hands together and standing on the tips of her toes. "It's a pyjama party. It's a sleepover.

It's *awesome*."

Dad said that just because we were having an American to stay, it did not give Iggy the right to speak like one.

"Aw, shucks," said Mum.

"Gee, can't we?" I said.

"OK, you guys," Dad said. "Enough already."

Dad's American accent is very good.

When they arrived, Uncle Chuck had to help Auntie Kate get out of the taxi because she was so big and round and pregnant. We all rushed out to meet them. Auntie Kate could hardly bend down for our kisses, because her baby got in the way. She waddled slowly in front of us up the path to the front door. She waddled like an Auntie-Kate-shaped penguin.

Iggy put her hand over her mouth and giggled.

"If you're wondering if I'm as uncomfortable as I look," Auntie Kate said, while she waddled, "the answer is *yes*."

Iggy stopped giggling. "Oh dear," she said. "Poor Auntie Kate."

"Ouch," said Dad.

"You can say that again," said Auntie Kate.

Auntie Kate made herself comfortable on the sofa, using all the cushions, and Mum brought her a cup of tea. Iggy and me sat on the floor, just underneath Auntie Kate's big round belly.

"When your baby comes," Iggy said, "will

I be an auntie like you?"

"You'll be the baby's cousins," Dad told her.

"Are cousins very important?" Iggy asked, sitting up straight like she does on the carpet at school.

"Definitely," said Auntie Kate. "Extremely important. Especially grown-up girl cousins, like you and Flo."

"Babysitters you mean," said Dad, and Auntie Kate smiled.

"Is it going to be a girl or a boy?" said Iggy. "Do you get to choose?"

"No, we don't get to choose and we don't even know yet. It will be a surprise."

"What are you going to call the baby?"

Iggy said. "Have you got any names?"

"Clover?" said Dad and Iggy blushed.

"Stella if it's a girl," Uncle Chuck said, "and Benjamin if it's a boy."

"When is he or she going to come?" Iggy said. "And where? And How? Can we be there?

"In a few weeks," said Auntie Kate. "In a big pool of water. As quickly and painlessly as possible."

"And no, you can't come," said Dad. "Having a baby is not a spectator sport."

"Absolutely not," said Mum.

"But can we see Stella or Benjamin as soon as she or he is born?" Iggy said.

"Sure you can," said Uncle Chuck.

"Who were the first people to meet us?" I said.

"We were," said Mum. "Me and Dad. And Flo was one of the first to meet you, Iggy."

I remember when Iggy was just born, even though I was only little. I remember she looked small and warm and pinkish, like a baked bean.

Auntie Kate grunted and shifted a bit on the sofa.

"I would very much like to have this baby soon," she said. "I miss sitting on a chair like a normal person. I feel like a beached whale."

"What's one of those?" Iggy said.

Kate said, "It's a whale who has come too far from the deep water where it swims and has got stuck on dry land and then realised how big and heavy and uncomfortable it is."

"How do you make a beached whale better?" I said.

"You keep them wet and you wait for the tide to come in, and when the water is deep enough they can swim away," said Uncle Chuck. "And sometimes you lift them with special machinery and put them back in the sea."

"Do you need lifting with special machinery?" Iggy asked Auntie Kate.

"Nearly," Auntie Kate said, and she tried to laugh, but her tummy got in the way.

In the night, there was a bit of a commotion. I heard voices and footsteps, and I heard the front door open and shut.

My heart was beating very fast, but I couldn't get up to see what was going on, because Iggy was asleep with one arm and one leg stretched across me. I didn't want to wake her up. Iggy snores very gently, like a small hippo.

In the morning, Iggy woke me up very gently, by tickling my face with her hair. When I opened my eyes, she was right there, close up and big, and smiling.

I was very tired.

"Shall we go and see people?" she whispered, still very close up.

"What people?"

"Auntie Kate and Uncle Chuck people!" Iggy said, climbing out of bed.

"In a minute," I said, turning over. "I'm not ready yet."

"Well, can you please be ready soon?" Iggy said, stretching up her arms until her belly button appeared from under her pyjama top.

I reached out and tickled it.

Iggy squeaked. "That feels *funny*," she said.

I told Iggy that Mum said belly buttons were the place where we used to be joined

to her by a cord when we were inside her tummy, like Auntie Kate's baby was inside hers. Iggy pulled up her top a bit and bent over to look at her belly button.

"What, there?" she said, sticking her finger in it.

"Yes, there. Mum said it's where they cut the cord and tie it in a knot when you first get born. They put a clip on it and it drops off."

Iggy put her hands on her hips. "You are making that up," she said.

"I'm not."

"You are."

"I promise," I told her.

Iggy looked once more at her belly button and once more at me, and then she got up.

"I'm asking Mum," she said.

Dad popped his head round the door.

"Asking Mum what?"

"About belly buttons," Iggy told him.

"She's not here," Dad said.

"Where is she?"

"She's gone with Auntie Kate and Uncle Chuck to have a baby."

Iggy shut her lips as tight as they would go and her eyes got bigger and bigger. She looked like she might explode.

I sat up in bed.

"But the baby isn't supposed to be born yet," I said.

"You and Auntie Kate and Uncle Chuck are about to find out that babies do whatever they want, never mind what's *supposed* to happen," said Dad.

"When did they go to have the baby?" I said. "And why did Mum go?"

"They went in the middle of the night," said Dad. "And Mum drove them to the hospital."

I remembered the voices and the footsteps and the sound of the front door.

"When will they be back?" I said.

"When they are ready."

"What do we do?" I asked.

"We wait for the phone to ring."

Iggy groaned.

It was a very long day. I had no idea it took such a long time to have a baby.

We had a cooked breakfast and got dressed and made our beds and tidied our rooms, but still no new baby.

We waited and waited and waited.

I wrote a Welcome to the World card, and Iggy wrote one too.

I made a changing mat out of four pieces of paper stuck together, with ducks and hearts and flowers all round the edge, and Iggy made one too.

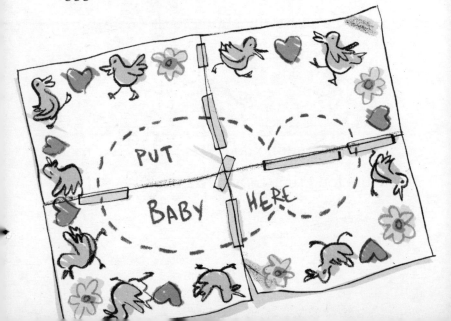

Still no new baby.

I drew a picture of Auntie Kate and Uncle Chuck and the new baby, and Iggy drew one too.

I asked Iggy quite politely not to copy me, and she said she couldn't help it because she was going mad with waiting and I had all the good ideas.

We watched TV, we played cards and we helped Dad with the recycling.

Still no new baby.

I thought the phone would never ring.

And then suddenly it did.

"Hello?" Dad said, and he listened, and

we held our breaths, and then he smiled.

"What? What is it? What?" Iggy said, jumping up and down.

"OK," Dad said. "See you in half an hour."

He put the phone down. He beamed. "It's a boy," he said.

"It's a Benjamin!" squeaked Iggy.

And then we were all jumping up and down and laughing and skipping about. We were just about as happy as we could be.

"Get your coats, girls," Dad said. "Let's go and meet the new Benjamin."

We went to the hospital. We kissed Benjamin's little pink nose and we counted his fingers

and toes and we gave him his Welcome to
the World cards.

"Hello, Benjamin," I said, putting my hand
on his warm tummy and feeling him wriggle.

"Hello, Benjamin," said Iggy, nuzzling his soft little head.

"Hello, Benjamin," we all said, while he slept, small and warm and pinkish, just like a baked bean, in Auntie Kate's arms.

"So, Iggy." Mum ruffled her hair. "You got what you wished for after all. This family has a brand new baby."

"Somebody smaller than you," Dad said.

"And he doesn't look at all noisy or hungry or smelly or exhausting," Iggy said.

"Just you wait," Dad told her. "Benjamin hasn't even got started yet."

I watched Iggy. She didn't say anything for a minute. She was unusually quiet. Iggy only goes quiet when she is up to no good or she is unspeakably happy. She covered her eyes with her hands. All we could see was her great big smile.

About the author

Jenny Valentine moved house every two years when she was growing up. She worked in a wholefood shop in Primrose Hill for fifteen years where she met many extraordinary people and sold more organic loaves than there are words in her first novel, *Finding Violet Park*, which won the Guardian Children's Fiction Prize. The *Iggy and Me* books are her first titles for younger readers.

About the illustrator

Joe Berger grew up in Bristol, where he did an Art Foundation Course before moving to London in 1991. He works as a freelance illustrator and animator, and also co-writes and illustrates a weekly comic strip in the *Guardian*. His first picture book, *Bridget Fidget*, was nominated for the Booktrust Early Years Award.

Find out more about Iggy and Me...

Iggy & Me: 9780007283620

Iggy & Me and
the Happy Birthday:
9780007283637

Iggy & Me on Holiday:
9780007283651